# S.P.I.S

SECRET. PROTECTION. INVESTIGATION. SOCIETY

ISSUE #1

"NEW RECRUIT"

CREATED, WRITTEN AND
ILLUSTRATED BY
DEION TILLETT

To order additional copies of this book, contact:
Xlibris
844-714-8691
www.Xlibris.com
Orders@Xlibris.com

ISBN:   Softcover        978-1-6698-1891-5
        EBook            978-1-6698-1892-2

Print information available on the last page

Rev. date: 03/31/2022

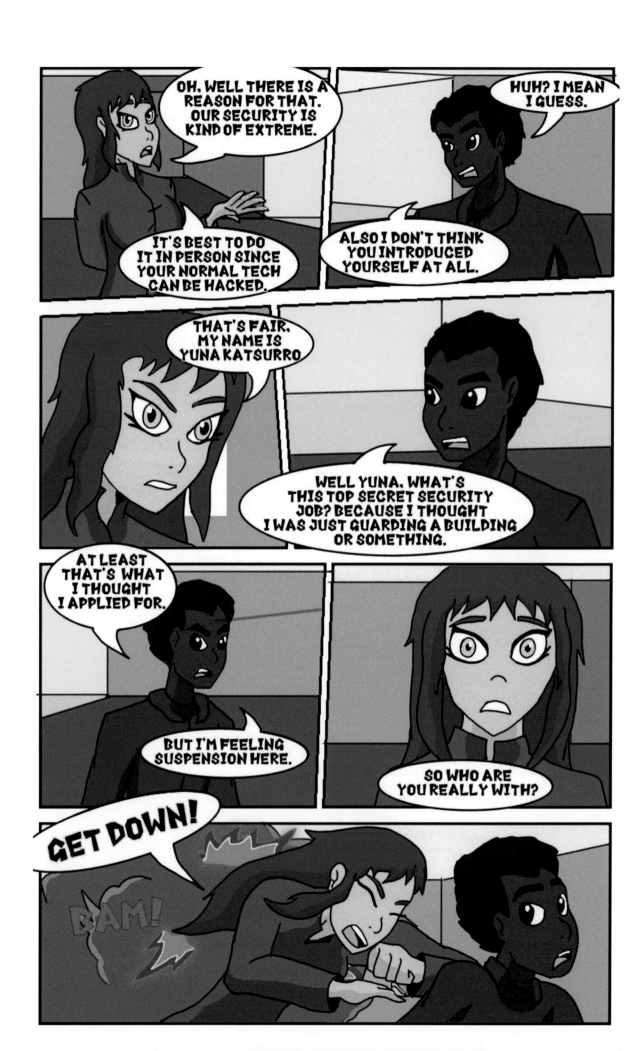

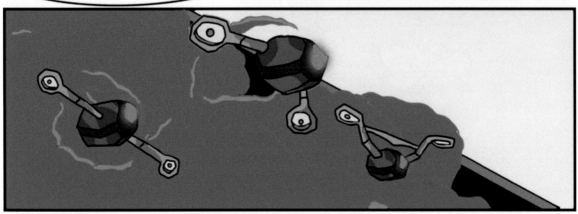

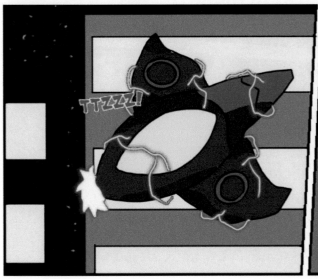

AQUILLO COMICS

ISSUE # 2

.I.S

SECRET, PROTECTION, INVESTIGATION, SOCIETY

NEXT ISSUE 6 " CHASE"

CREATED, WRITTEN AND
ILLUSTRATED BY
DEION TILLETT

Printed in the United States
by Baker & Taylor Publisher Services